Susanna Davidson

Designed by Karen Tomlins

History consultant: Heather Thomas
Reading consultant: Alison Kelly

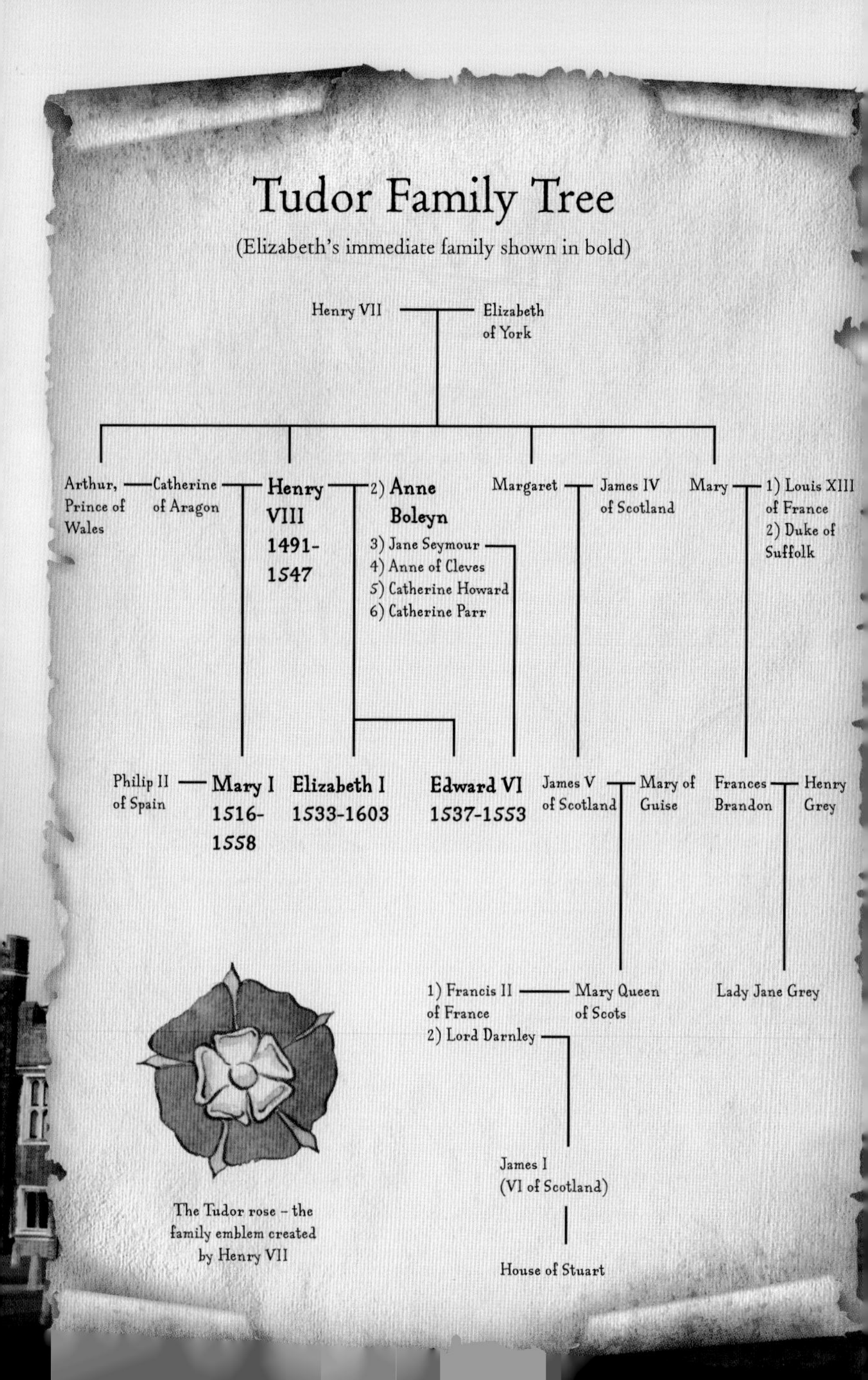
Tudor Family Tree
(Elizabeth's immediate family shown in bold)
Henry VII
Elizabeth of York
Arthur, Prince of Wales
Catherine of Aragon
Henry VIII 1491-1547
2) Anne Boleyn
3) Jane Seymour
4) Anne of Cleves
5) Catherine Howard
6) Catherine Parr
Margaret
James IV of Scotland
Mary
1) Louis XIII of France
2) Duke of Suffolk
Philip II of Spain
Mary I 1516-1558
Elizabeth I 1533-1603
Edward VI 1537-1553
James V of Scotland
Mary of Guise
Frances Brandon
Henry Grey
1) Francis II of France
2) Lord Darnley
Mary Queen of Scots
Lady Jane Grey
James I (VI of Scotland)
House of Stuart
The Tudor rose – the family emblem created by Henry VII

Contents

Hampton Court Palace – one of Elizabeth's many homes once she became queen

Chapter 1

Lady Elizabeth

Elizabeth stood in the gardens of Hunsdon House, a puzzled expression on her face. "Why was I addressed as my Lady Princess yesterday," she asked her governor, "and only as Lady Elizabeth today?"

She was just three years old, but Elizabeth knew she was a princess. Her father was Henry VIII, England's greatest king, and she had his fair skin and red hair to prove it. Elizabeth thought of him like the sun, a glorious, and distant figure, who could toss her up in the air laughing, or silence her with a lash of his fiery tongue.

Elizabeth's father, King Henry VIII

Elizabeth's mother, Anne Boleyn, in a stylish French hood

But she had her coal black eyes from her mother, Queen Anne, who sent her parcels stuffed with beautiful clothes... although there had been none for a while now. Her nurse, Lady Bryan had tutted over it, grumbling that soon she'd have nothing left to wear. Something was changing, Elizabeth was sure of it, and no one would tell her what it was.

"You're not a princess any more," was all she got in reply. "You're just a lady now, like your sister, Lady Mary."

The truth was a hard thing to tell a little girl – that her mother, the King's second wife, was dead, beheaded at the Tower of London, on trumped up charges of plotting to kill the King. Elizabeth had been banned from ever becoming queen. It was as if her parents' marriage had never been. Her father had fallen in love again and wanted nothing more to do with his daughter.

Lady Mary Tudor, Elizabeth's half-sister

The closest thing Elizabeth had to a parent now was her half-sister, Lady Mary, who was seventeen years her senior.

For a long time Mary had resented Elizabeth, blaming Elizabeth's mother, Anne, for stealing away her father's affections, and for causing her parents' divorce. But now the half-sisters were in the same position: motherless, cut off from their father's affection, barred from the throne.

Lady Mary felt pity stir in her heart and brought her little sister gifts of pocket money, necklaces, brooches... a box embroidered with silver.

More changes were to come. "You have a new baby brother, Edward," Lady Bryan told Elizabeth, shortly after her fourth birthday. King Henry had married again, for the third time, and at last had his longed-for son. But even as the King rejoiced at having an heir, his wife died, only two weeks after giving birth. Elizabeth was horrified to discover Lady Bryan was to look after Edward.

This 19th-century painting shows a one year old Prince Edward in his royal nursery.

"But what about *me*?" she demanded.

It was the moment a young woman called Kat Ashley swept into her life, becoming her governess, and her friend. Kat cared for Elizabeth, loved her dearly and taught her everything she knew... mathematics, geography, astronomy, architecture, history needlework, dancing and riding. Elizabeth loved learning and Kat delighted in her quickness.

At the age of six, Elizabeth was impressing the King's future royal secretary with her knowledge. "She has the assurance of a woman of forty," he reported to the palace, "already learned enough to make her father proud."

As soon as Edward was old enough to have tutors of his own, Elizabeth shared them with him, so that her lessons now included Latin, Greek, Italian handwriting and French.

To amuse themselves, Edward and Elizabeth rode out in the royal parks, went hunting and walking, watched bear-baiting and cock-fights. They also had an army of servants just for their entertainment – minstrels, players and fools. They moved between the royal houses of Hertfordshire, the King and his Court seeming very far away. But her father's actions continued to shock. In February 1542, when

Elizabeth was eight, her father had his fifth wife, Catherine Howard, beheaded at the Tower, just like Elizabeth's mother before her.

"I will never marry," Elizabeth vowed to her friend, Robert Dudley, on hearing the news. It was clear to her now that marriage could all too easily go hand in hand with death.

Hertford Castle Gatehouse – all that remains of the castle where Elizabeth spent much of her childhood

Chapter 2

Death and danger

Ever since her mother's death, Elizabeth had been an outsider in the royal family, invited to Court only on the occasional whim of her father or stepmother. But here she was, eight years old, with a letter in her hand inviting her and Mary to dine with their father. This was Elizabeth's chance to win her father back.

Elizabeth and Mary were to go by carriage to Pyrgo Park, the royal hunting lodge in Essex.

Elizabeth, dressed in her finest clothes, put on the performance of her life. She used the conversation to show off her knowledge of the Bible, Latin, Greek, anything that would encourage her father to think of her as his daughter again. *Had she done enough?* she worried on the journey home, her long white fingers playing on her sleeve.

It seemed that she had. Eight months later, she and Mary were invited to Court to meet their father's future wife, Catherine Parr, and were guests of honour at the wedding. The following year, they were restored to their place in the succession.

'The Family of Henry VIII' was commissioned by Henry to celebrate his decision to restore his daughters to the succession. Mary is on the far left, Edward and his mother, Jane Seymour, are either side of Henry. Elizabeth is on the far right.

Elizabeth knew it was unlikely she would ever be queen: first Edward, then Mary would inherit the throne, and both would have to die childless for that to happen. But she was in line to the throne again, and one of the most important ladies in the land. There was a ceremony to mark the occasion, a grand dinner at Whitehall, followed by a huge gathering with wine and sweetmeats. All the most important people were invited and, at last, Elizabeth was able to bask in her father's affection and approval.

But soon after being re-united with her father, Elizabeth risked losing him once more. He left for war in France, determined to win a great victory for England. All Elizabeth could do was pray fervently for his safe return.

She couldn't help but be excited by the change in her life. From the age of eleven, she was allowed to stay at Court. With avid curiosity, she watched Queen Catherine ruling in her father's absence.

A portrait of Catherine Parr, Henry VIII's sixth, and last, wife

The most powerful men in the land would come and bow low before her, making Elizabeth wonder... would it be possible, after all, for a queen to rule instead of a king?

There was a buzz around Catherine's court too, for those who were caught up in a fever of religious learning. Twelve years earlier, the King had broken with the Pope in Rome and made himself Supreme Head of the Church in England. Most people were still Catholics, their churches decorated with paintings and statues, lit by candles and infused with incense. But the King's new wife, Catherine, had a different faith – she was secretly becoming a Protestant. Elizabeth listened in wide-eyed wonder to the chaplains who came, each afternoon, to preach in the Queen's privy chamber.

For the next two years, Elizabeth lived the life she had always dreamed of – in the beautiful countryside of Hertfordshire, often with Edward at her side, competing for the admiration of their tutors, with thrilling visits to Court. One of her tutors, Roger Ascham, declared he had never known a girl who learned so quickly, or with a better memory. "Of all the ladies in the land," he claimed, "the brightest star is my illustrious Lady Elizabeth."

She was becoming fluent in Latin, French and Greek, as well as learning Italian, Welsh, philosophy and history. She could sing and write music, and play the lute and virginals.

When her father returned from war in France, she was there to greet him with the rest of her family. At last she felt secure in his affection. "Matchless and most benevolent father..." she wrote to him at Christmas.

As she grew older, she was allowed to come to Court more and more frequently. Her visits were only marred by her realization that her father's health was deteriorating, fast. She watched him

struggling to walk, dragged along the endless palace corridors in a special wheeled chair, his face black and breathless.

Shortly after Christmas, a surprise party came to see her at the Palace of Enfield, where she was staying. It was Edward, and his uncle, the Earl of Hertford. Once he had them together, Hertford broke the news that their father was dead. Edward and Elizabeth broke down in sobs, but they had little time to share their grief. Hertford left for London with Edward, who had become king at just nine years old. Elizabeth and Edward would never be so close again.

Edward's coronation procession in 1547 – on the left, you can see the Tower and old London Bridge

Although her father had left her money in his will, at fourteen she was too young to live on her own. So she went to live with her stepmother, Catherine, in London.

But just three months after Henry's death, Catherine married again, to Thomas Seymour, one of the King's uncles. He was tall and dashing with auburn hair, and he soon began to flirt with Elizabeth, who blushed whenever his name was mentioned. Catherine seemed to think nothing of it, but Kat Ashley was outraged. "Think of your reputation," she told Elizabeth, fearing that Elizabeth was falling in love with him. But soon, even Catherine decided things were going too far, and she sent Elizabeth away, to stay with Kat's sister and her husband.

Elizabeth wrote frequently, wishing Catherine, who was now heavily pregnant, 'a most lucky deliverance'. But it was not to be. Three days after the birth of her daughter, Catherine fell ill with a fever and died. Seymour quickly turned his attentions back to Elizabeth, this time with the intention of marrying her. After all, she was an heir

This portrait of Lady Elizabeth – a book in her hands and a Bible on the lectern behind her – was probably done for Henry VIII in the last few months of his life.

to the throne, and a source of wealth and power. Seymour was also plotting to overthrow his older brother, who was ruling the country on behalf of the child-king. Seymour had decided to try to kidnap the King, and rule the country himself.

One night, Seymour crept into the King's palace. When King Edward's pet spaniel started to bark at him, he shot the dog, was arrested, and taken to the Tower. There, his plans to marry Elizabeth leaked out. Shortly afterwards, Kat Ashley and another of Elizabeth's servants were taken to the Tower, while others were sent to interrogate Elizabeth.

Under questioning, Elizabeth broke down and cried. She admitted to Seymour's interest in her, but nothing more, swearing she would "never... marry, either in England nor out of England, without the consent of the King..."

Sir Thomas Seymour, whose plans to marry Elizabeth put her life in danger

She knew she must escape scandal. She was fighting for her reputation.

Elizabeth fought hard for her servants too, demanding they be released from the Tower. "The love she hath to Ashley," noted her questioner, "is to be wondered at." There was nothing she could do for Seymour, and two weeks later he was executed. "This day died a man of much wit and very little judgement," she said, knowing to say more would be to risk her own head. He was her first love, and he had been beheaded.

Even after Seymour's death, Elizabeth was dogged by gossip and slander. People said she had secretly given birth to Thomas Seymour's child, but Elizabeth was quick to defend herself. She began to live quietly, dressing plainly, determined to save her name. Edward, still fond of Elizabeth, called her his 'sweet sister temperance'. Although his new position as King stood between them, they were bound together by their shared Protestant beliefs.

But then, in the winter of 1552, Edward fell ill. By the following spring it was clear he would not live long. Coughing up black mucus, he lay pale and wasted in his bed.

By law, the throne should have passed to Edward's

elder sister Mary, but she was a Catholic and Edward, fervently religious himself, wanted the crown to go to a Protestant. He wrote a will, cutting Mary out of the succession. Possibly under pressure, and to justify his actions, he cut out Elizabeth too, and named his cousin, Lady Jane Grey, as his rightful heir. Four days after his death, Lady Jane Grey was brought to the Tower of London and proclaimed Queen. But it was not to last...

A painting of Lady Jane Grey, also known as the 'Nine Days Queen'

Queen Mary in 1554, a year after she came to the throne

Mary knew the people supported her and fought back for what she saw as her birthright. She raised an army, marched on London and began preparing for her coronation. Elizabeth had been waiting quietly at her home at Hatfield, watching to see what would happen. As soon as Mary was crowned, she wrote to congratulate her, then rode to greet her. She came with an escort of 2,000 horses, her men dressed in her father's green and white livery. There had been plottings and intrigues, but Elizabeth had survived.

Chapter 3

To the Tower

Mary began by being friendly – holding Elizabeth's hand affectionately, asking her to appear in public at her side. But, all too soon, religion and the past rose up between them. Mary insisted Elizabeth come to Catholic mass with her,

Queen Mary and Lady Elizabeth entering London side by side, after Mary's accession to the throne

which Elizabeth tried to avoid. The more Mary looked at Elizabeth, the more she remembered Elizabeth's mother, Anne Boleyn, and all the suffering she had caused. Her advisors warned Mary against Elizabeth, describing her as clever and sly and possessed of 'a spirit full of enchantment.' They urged Mary to send Elizabeth to the Tower, or at least away from Court, warning that she could be a focus for discontented Protestants.

Mary was convinced, now, that Elizabeth should never inherit the throne. She couldn't bear to see it pass to a Protestant and she refused to believe Elizabeth when she said she was a true Catholic. Instead, Mary was determined to marry, and produce an heir of her own. She settled on Prince Philip of Spain as her future husband. It was to be a fatal choice.

As the news spread, Mary's popularity plummeted. The people were horrified by the proposed marriage, loathing the idea of a Spanish ruler taking over, dragging them into foreign wars. Spain was a powerful country with a vast empire, and many feared that if Prince Philip married their Queen, England would lose its independence.

Thomas Wyatt, whose failed rebellion against Mary led to his execution in 1554

One man, Sir Thomas Wyatt, decided it was time to rebel. He planned to march on London to stop the marriage and wrote to Elizabeth, asking for her help.

Mary's supporters began to suspect Elizabeth of being involved in some kind of plot. When Elizabeth asked to leave Court, Mary reluctantly agreed, but was sure her sister would, "bring about some great evil unless she is dealt with." She gave orders for spies to be placed in her household to watch her every move. On parting, the sisters embraced, Elizabeth begging Mary not to believe, "anyone who spread evil reports of her," but Mary was still suspicious.

In January 1554, after the marriage treaty had been signed, Wyatt marched on London, with a rebel army 5,000 strong. Mary immediately wrote to Elizabeth, demanding she come to Court. She didn't say it in the letter, but she wanted to keep an eye on her sister.

Elizabeth replied that she was too ill to travel, having, "such a cold and headache that I never felt the like." This only confirmed Mary's suspicions that Elizabeth was involved. The rebellion failed, but the threat and fear of it hardened Mary's heart. Lady Jane Grey, who had been imprisoned in the Tower all this time, was now seen as too much of a threat. She was executed, along with the leaders of the rebellion. Then Mary turned her attention to Elizabeth, sending three councillors and two doctors to bring her to London, provided she could be safely moved.

A painting of the execution of Lady Jane Grey. The straw on the floor was to soak up the blood.

A marriage portrait of King Philip II of Spain and Queen Mary

Elizabeth did all she could not to come, pleading that she was still unwell and not yet strong enough to make the journey. But this time, Mary would hear no excuses. Elizabeth became sicker still, her illness brought on by fear. When she arrived in London, she begged to see Mary, but Mary refused. Instead, Elizabeth was questioned closely about her involvement in the rebellion. "You must admit your guilt," she was told, "or you will suffer the severest penalty."

Elizabeth would not admit to any guilt and was told, to her horror, that she was to be sent to the Tower. She believed she would meet her end there, just as her mother and Lady Jane Grey had before her.

When she was ordered to step onto the boat, to take her to the Tower, Elizabeth tried everything she could to delay it. "Wait for the next tide," she begged, desperate for one more day of freedom. She was refused. "Then let me write a letter," she asked. At last they agreed to that, and Elizabeth sat down to write a letter to her sister – a letter begging for her life. "Kneeling with humbleness of heart," she wrote, "... I humbly crave to speak with Your Highness... I know myself most true. As for the traitor Wyatt, he might... write me a letter, but on my faith I never received any from him..."

Elizabeth's handwriting became a frantic scribble. She came to a halt near the top of a page, but couldn't bear to leave any space in case her enemies put their own words there. She scratched heavy diagonal lines across the rest of the page, then at the bottom, she put, "I humbly crave but one word of answer from yourself. Your Highness's most faithful subject that hath been from the beginning and will be to my end, Elizabeth."

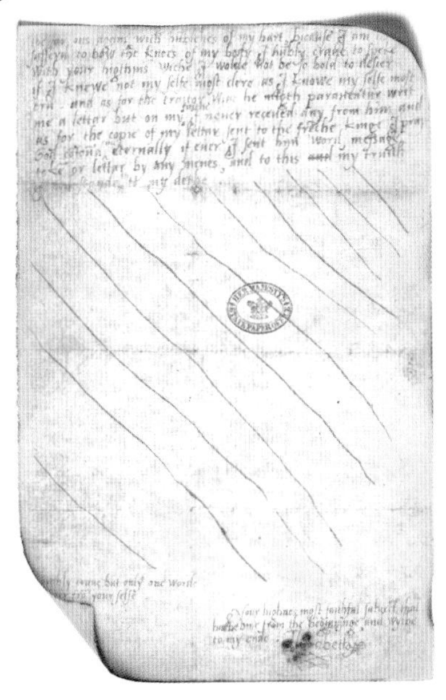

The last page of Elizabeth's letter to Mary – clearly showing the heavy lines scratched across the page

By the time she had finished the letter, the tide had turned. Elizabeth had gained a day, but Mary refused even to read the letter. In a moment, Elizabeth had gone from the second most important lady in the land, to a prisoner in fear of her life.

Elizabeth's rooms in the tower were well-furnished, but she was forbidden to leave them. Again, she was closely questioned about her knowledge of the plot, but there wasn't enough evidence against her.

This engraving shows the Tower of London from the River Thames. Elizabeth entered via Traitor's Gate, which you can see at the water line.

Elizabeth's fear, however, was very real. She even thought of asking the Queen if she could be beheaded by a swordsman, as her mother had been, rather than face a slower death by an axe.

Mary's councillors were still divided over what to do with Elizabeth. At last, it was decided she should be put under house arrest, at Woodstock, in the care of Sir Henry Bedingfield.

As she was transported away from London, the people came out in her support. Church bells were rung in celebration of her release, and people cried out, "God save your Grace!"

Lady Elizabeth was taken to the Tower on March 18, 1554, and imprisoned in the Bell Tower until May 19.

At first, Elizabeth suspected that Mary would secretly attempt to have her murdered, but after a few weeks of house arrest, she realized her life was no longer in danger.

While Elizabeth waited impatiently at Woodstock, Mary's popularity was foundering. She had married Philip and was persecuting Protestants, inflaming even more anger against her. She thought her prayers had been answered when it looked as if she

An engraving showing the burning of Protestants, under Mary's orders, at Smithfield, London, in 1553

had at last become pregnant, but her pregnancy turned out to be no more than wishful thinking. People began to ridicule her openly. King Philip, convinced that Mary would never bear him an heir, left to attend to the rest of his empire. Mary was heartbroken.

In October 1555, Elizabeth was at last allowed to return to Hatfield. But her relationship with Mary didn't recover: Mary remained convinced Elizabeth was still a threat.

Elizabeth had a new ally, however, in Mary's husband, Philip, who saw Elizabeth as the future heir to the throne. He refused to let Mary send Elizabeth back to the Tower, or cut her out of the succession – even when it looked as if Elizabeth, or at least her servants, were plotting against Mary.

The Queen's health worsened, and without a child to name as her heir, people began to look forward to the day Elizabeth would take the throne. Just as everyone had feared, King Philip had dragged England into a war against France. England lost its last piece of land in France – Calais – and the cost of the war had drained the country of money. Mary was now deeply unpopular.

By November 1558, it was clear that Mary was dying. She finally agreed to name Elizabeth as her successor, asking only that she continue in the Catholic faith. Elizabeth was poised to take over. She had secretly arranged with one of Mary's councillors that he would come to her the moment Mary died, bringing with him Mary's betrothal ring as proof.

A photograph of the Old Palace of Hatfield, Hertfordshire, which still stands today. It was here that Elizabeth heard the news of Mary's death.

Elizabeth was in the gardens of Hatfield when she heard the news. At first, she was speechless. Then she sank to the ground, saying in Latin, "This is the Lord's doing: it is marvellous in our eyes."

No one challenged Elizabeth's right to rule. After so long on the edges of power, always fearing for her life, it took just six hours from Mary's death for Elizabeth, now 25, to be declared Queen of England.

Chapter 4

Queen at last

On the morning of her coronation, January 15, 1559, Elizabeth was dressed in her robes: a swirling silk cloak lined with ermine and patterned with Tudor roses, the proud symbol of her royal family line. She had spent the last two months in London, parading before her people. On winter evenings, she could be seen in her barge, being rowed along the Thames to the sound of music.

The day before, on her coronation eve, the City had celebrated their new queen with pageants, fanfares and singing. Elizabeth had accepted gifts offered by the poor – posies of flowers, a spray of rosemary. She had listened to children reciting poems and waved to the crowds. "God save them all!" she had cried, again and again, to those who welcomed her. "I will be as good unto you as ever a queen was to her people."

Elizabeth's coronation robes had to be prepared in a hurry. There wasn't enough time to make new robes, so Elizabeth simply used Mary's, but had the bodice and sleeves remade.

Now the moment had come for her to take her oath. She went in procession to Westminster Abbey, which glowed with the light of hundreds of candles. During the ceremony, there was shouting and cheering, trumpets and bells. Afterwards, wearing a crown and carrying the orb and sceptre, she walked out to greet her people, smiling at the crowds. Elizabeth's reign had begun.

Ten days later, at her first Parliament, her ministers made it clear they wanted Elizabeth to marry, and as soon as possible. Women, they claimed, were unfit for power in a world dominated by men. Parliament reminded Elizabeth it would be better for her, "and her kingdom if she would take a consort who might relieve her of those labours which are only fit for men."

An engraving showing Queen Elizabeth I, on her throne, attending Parliament

"I am already bound unto a husband," Elizabeth replied, "which is the kingdom of England." Elizabeth had no wish to marry. She was all too aware that a foreign prince could drag England into a costly war, and if she married one of her subjects, it would create rivalries at Court. Above all, she had no desire to lose her new-found freedom. She meant to rule by herself.

But even as she was refusing offers of marriage, and playing off one foreign suitor against another, many believed Elizabeth to be in love with her childhood friend, Lord Robert Dudley. Tall and handsome, with dark skin, red-brown hair and heavy-lidded eyes, Elizabeth made no secret of

A painting of Elizabeth and Dudley dancing the 'La Volta', thought to be a very daring dance at the time

her affection for him, calling him her 'bonny sweet Robin'. She consulted him on state affairs, rode with him on horseback, hunted and danced with him. And as he already had a wife, Elizabeth could enjoy his company without having to commit herself to marriage.

As gossip about them spread, Kat Ashley begged Elizabeth to put some distance between them. Elizabeth refused to listen, instead granting Dudley more and more privileges. Then, in September 1560, to Elizabeth's horror, Dudley's wife, Amy, was found dead at her home in Cumnor Place, Oxfordshire, her neck apparently broken by a fall down a shallow flight of stairs. Even after her death was pronounced an accident, many people believed that Robert Dudley had arranged for his wife to be murdered, so that he could marry the Queen.

This painting entitled 'The Death of Amy Robsart' shows Dudley's wife dead, at the bottom of the stairs.

Some even said that Elizabeth had been an accomplice. Elizabeth was furious, but she still refused to distance herself from Dudley. The scandal and gossip became more and more heated, as everyone waited to see what would happen next. Whatever Elizabeth's feelings, she knew that to marry Dudley would threaten her reign, as well as her independence. In November, she promised to make him an earl, but at the ceremony she took a knife and cut up the documents in front of him. She was showing the world that she was in control of her feelings. Never again, when it came to the question of marriage, would Elizabeth allow her heart to rule her head.

But by refusing to marry and have children, her councillors remained troubled by the question of who would be her heir. They were more worried than ever in October 1562, when Elizabeth fell dangerously ill with smallpox. "Death possessed every joint of me," she said afterwards.

Much to their relief, the Queen made a rapid recovery. But they were aware that waiting in the wings was another queen, who considered the English throne rightfully hers, and was busy plotting to make it her own.

Chapter 5

Rivals

Mary Stuart, Queen of Scotland, was Elizabeth's first cousin. She had been married to the King of France, but returned home when he died in 1560. Mary's reappearance was to cause Elizabeth eighteen years of trouble.

Since the beginning of her reign, Elizabeth had made it clear she was steering the country towards Protestantism. But Mary Stuart was a Catholic and many Catholics, both at home and abroad, looked to her as their hope of restoring the Catholic religion in England.

Mary was desperate for Elizabeth to name her as her successor. But Elizabeth believed that to do so would be to 'bury herself alive', undermining her power and encouraging others to conspire against her. Elizabeth was all the more furious when Mary refused to give up her claims to the English throne.

The two remained friendly, however, until 1565, when Mary married her cousin, Henry Darnley, against Elizabeth's wishes.

Darnley also had a claim to the English throne, and together they presented an even greater threat. But unlike Elizabeth, Mary allowed her emotions to cloud her judgement.

A portrait of Mary Stuart, also Mary I of Scotland, Elizabeth's cousin and rival

Mary and Darnley had a son, James, but the marriage soon soured, and Mary made it all too clear she wished to be rid of her husband. A few months later, an explosion tore through the house where Darnley had been staying. When they found his body, marks on this throat showed that he had been strangled. It looked as if the explosion had been a cover up for murder, and fingers began to point to Mary. Elizabeth was horrified: "Madam," she wrote to Mary, "my ears have been so astounded and my heart so frightened to hear of the horrible and abominable murder of your husband..."

But Mary went further. Two months later she was 'abducted' by the man suspected of her husband's murder – James Bothwell – and married him.

The Scottish lords fought Bothwell and led Mary back to Edinburgh, to cries from the people of, "Kill her! Drown her!" Imprisoned, she was forced to abdicate to her infant son, who became James VI of Scotland.

Whatever Elizabeth thought of Mary's conduct, she hated the idea of a queen being captured by her people, and fought hard for her release.

A year later, Mary fled to England, seeking refuge. But her presence threw Elizabeth into turmoil. She couldn't send Mary back to Scotland, to face certain death. But nor did she want Mary in England, as a focus for Catholic rebellion.

Mary Stuart escaping from Loch Leven Castle, where she had been imprisoned

Instead she decided to keep Mary as her 'guest', under constant observation.

"The Queen of Scots," warned William Cecil, Elizabeth's councillor, "is, and always shall be, a dangerous person to your estate."

William Cecil, who became Elizabeth's most trusted advisor for forty years, from 1558 until his death in 1598

Just as Cecil had predicted, and Elizabeth feared, Mary became a focus of rebellion and discontent. The Duke of Norfolk, one of the most powerful noblemen in the country, wanted to marry Mary, so that together they could claim the throne. Rebellion was brewing in the north, too, where many English Catholics were plotting to depose Elizabeth and replace her with Mary.

Elizabeth imprisoned Norfolk in the Tower, but the rebels from the north began to march south, hoping to reach Tutbury, where Mary Stuart was held.

As soon as she heard of the uprising, Elizabeth gave orders for Mary to be moved and guarded even more carefully. A month later, the rebellion collapsed. In her fury, Elizabeth had many of the rebels executed.

Over the next few years, Mary plotted continuously. When she realized she could never return to Scotland, she declared: "I will not leave my prison save as Queen of England."

To protect Elizabeth, William Cecil put in place a spy network, headed by Francis Walsingham, to intercept many of Mary's letters. Walsingham's patience was at last rewarded, when his spies

In captivity, Mary had her own servants, her rooms were decorated with fine tapestries – but she was rarely allowed out.

Babington with his fellow plotters in St. Giles Fields, London, in 1586

deciphered a letter in which Mary gave her consent to the 'Babington plot'. Anthony Babington, a rich Catholic, and six other men, were to 'despatch the usurper' Elizabeth, rescue Mary and, with the help of Spanish forces, put her on the English throne.

Cecil moved quickly to arrest the rebels. When the news was made public, the bells of London rang in celebration and people gave thanks, lit bonfires and held street parties.

Both Elizabeth's councillors and her parliament demanded that Mary should be punished, just as the other plotters had been. Elizabeth still wanted to spare Mary's life, if only because she hated the thought of executing another queen. But her councillors insisted that she owed it to her people to make the kingdom safe.

The decision brought Elizabeth close to breakdown. At last, after much prevaricating, she signed the death warrant. On February 8, 1587, Mary was brought into the Great Hall of Fotheringhay Castle, watched by 300 spectators.

Now 44 years old, plump, double-chinned, grey-haired and lame, she carried herself with dignity, dressed in a black satin gown. She knelt and lay her head on the block, praying in Latin, "Into Thy hands, O Lord, I commend my spirit." It took two blows of the axe to sever her head.

The people rejoiced that a traitor had died, but Elizabeth did not. She became hysterical, partly with grief, partly through fear that God would punish her for what she had done. She looked around for someone else to blame and accused Davison, one of her councillors, of submitting the death warrant without her approval. He was fined and imprisoned in the Tower. Catholic Europe blamed Elizabeth for what she had done, but no one made a move against her.

By April, Elizabeth had forgiven Davison and the other coucillors who had pleaded for Mary's death.

She felt relieved that at last the Catholic cause no longer had its claimant to the crown. Once again, Elizabeth had come face to face with danger and survived.

Right: the death warrant for Mary Stuart, signed by Elizabeth

Below: a painting of Mary, in her widow's clothes and white veil, walking towards the executioner's block

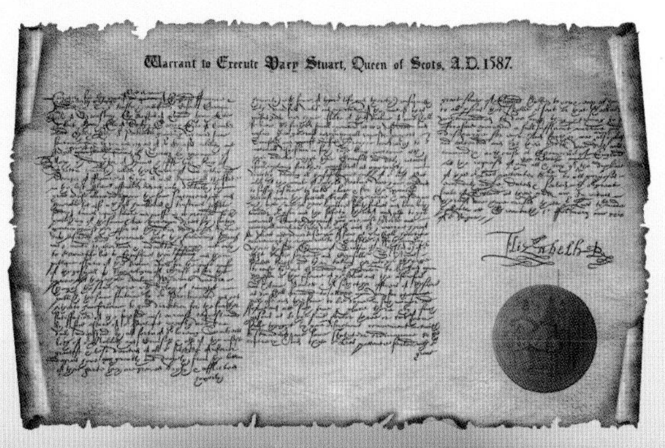

Warrant to Execute Mary Stuart, Queen of Scots, A.D. 1587.

A portrait of Queen Elizabeth, dated 1588

Chapter 6

Gloriana

By now, Elizabeth had reigned peacefully for twenty-nine years. She believed God had brought her to the throne, and attributed her 'happy reign... to God alone'. She saw herself as a mother to her people, and she felt the need, more than anything, to be loved by them.

Elizabeth encouraged the image of herself as the Virgin Queen, married to her kingdom and her people. The poets and dramatists of the day added to the cult. The poet Edmund Spenser called her 'Gloriana'; William Shakespeare and Ben Johnson referred to her as Diana, 'Queen and huntress, chaste and fair'. In turn, she gave them her patronage, formed her own company of players, the Queen's Men, and paid for their plays to be performed at Court.

A painting depicting the playwright Shakespeare reading to Queen Elizabeth

Elizabeth also understood the need to see her people and be seen by them. Every year, unless there was an outbreak of the plague, she made a lavish tour around the country. "We princes are set as it were upon stages in the sight of the world," she observed.

But the realities of Elizabeth's life were far less glamorous. "To be a king and wear a crown is more glorious to them that see it than it is a pleasure to them that bear it," she once said. She was always surrounded by others – her ladies of the bedchamber at night, and her courtiers by day. Her hours were filled with writing letters, receiving petitions and deciding what should be brought before the Council. She usually worked late into the night, talking to ministers.

But Elizabeth had the energy for the task. She excelled at hunting, dancing and music, and still found the time to study, often choosing to read history and philosophy

Elizabeth's passion for the lute meant that all noblemen were expected to be able to play it.

texts in her spare hours, or translating works from Latin and Ancient Greek.

She could be kind and generous to friends, but was also known for her vicious temper and her rages. She boxed the ears of her maids and even went so far as to punch a councillor who displeased her.

Elizabeth was cautious when it came to ruling her country, avoiding war, which she thought could only threaten England's wealth and stability. But peace with a hostile, Catholic Europe was a hard thing to achieve. The year after Mary's execution, England began to brace itself for war with Spain.

King Philip had decided to send his Armada – his fleet of Spanish galleons – to defeat the English navy. The ships would then pick up Spanish troops, waiting at Calais under the Duke of Parma, before returning to England to invade.

On July 19, 1588, the Spanish Armada was sighted approaching the English coast. The Queen reacted calmly, while the nation waited, expectant and fearful. The fleet was ready, flying the Tudor white and green flags from its masts, under the command of Sir Francis Drake.

At midnight on July 28, they sent five fire-ships, packed with burning wood and pitch, to sail between the Spanish galleons. The galleons scattered before the flames, then found themselves unable to regroup because of the strong winds. At that moment, the English fleet began to fight against them. In the battle that raged over the next few days, the Spanish lost eleven ships and 2,000 men, while the English lost just fifty men and none of their ships. Then the winds changed, forcing the Armada northwards, scattering the remaining ships and wrecking many more along the coast.

But Elizabeth wasn't ready to rejoice. Parma's army might still invade as soon as the winds were right. Elizabeth went to rally her troops. Wearing a silver breastplate, she gave a rousing speech. "I am come amongst you all," she told them, "not for my

recreation and disport, but being resolved in the midst and heat of the battle to live and die amongst you all... I know I have the body of a weak and feeble woman, but I have the heart and stomach of a king, and of a king of England too..."

The soldiers gave a mighty cheer. News soon came that Parma and his army were due to set sail. Elizabeth's councillors urged her to return to London for safety, but she refused. Then, as night approached, they discovered the danger had passed. Parma had refused to come without help from the Spanish navy. Elizabeth rode back to London in triumph. The Spanish ambassador reported that she had not lost her presence of mind for a single moment.

The launching of English fire-ships against the Spanish Armada

This was the high point of her reign. Since the defeat of the Armada, Elizabeth had become one of the most respected monarchs in Europe, even by her enemies. "Just look how well she governs!" said the Pope. "She is only a woman, only mistress of half an island, and yet she makes herself feared by Spain, by France, by the Empire, by all!" The national spirit was buoyed with confidence.

On the world stage, England had become famous for its explorers. Among them was Sir Francis Drake, who plundered Spanish treasure ships and circumnavigated the world, and Sir Walter Raleigh, who discovered Guyana.

A replica of *The Golden Hinde*, the ship used by explorer Sir Francis Drake

Sir Francis Drake

Both were funded and encouraged by Elizabeth, and it was Raleigh who suggested the English settlement in North America be named Virginia, after the Virgin Queen.

A 16th century map detailing Sir Walter Raleigh's arrival in Virginia

Elizabeth was becoming a legend in her own lifetime. Raleigh, a poet as well as an explorer, wrote of her:

To seek new worlds for gold, for praise, for glory,
To try desire, to try love severed far,
When I was gone, she sent her memory,
More strong than were ten thousand ships of war...

Chapter 7

The final years

By 1590, Elizabeth's Court was beginning to change. Most of her old friends and councillors were dying or retiring. A month after the Armada, Elizabeth was griefstricken by the death of Robert Dudley. Although he had married again, he had remained close to her, and for thirty years had been 'her brother and best friend'. She placed his last letter in a little box by her bed, where it was found after her death.

After the blow of Dudley's death, came Sir Francis Walsingham's, her 'spymaster', followed by Blanche Parry, her old nurse. Her chief advisor, William Cecil, ill with gout, begged to be allowed to retire, but Elizabeth refused to let him. Then, in 1591, she was plunged into grief by the death of another councillor, Sir Christopher Hatton. And all around her, new factions were springing up at Court, mostly divided between those who followed Cecil's son, Robert, and Dudley's stepson, Robert Devereux, the Earl of Essex.

Essex was volatile and passionate. The Queen adored and indulged him, although they frequently clashed, as Essex's lust for power grew. His moment for glory came when he carried out a successful raid on the Spanish port of Cadiz. Elizabeth wrote, "You have made me famous, dreadful and renowned, not more for your victory than for your courage." At home, people celebrated his achievements, which in turn made Elizabeth jealous of his popularity.

She jealously guarded her fading beauty, too. In the 1590s she discovered portraits of herself with a sagging chin and cheeks, which she ordered to be destroyed, along with any others that showed her looking old, frail and ill.

This is a portrait of Robert Devereux, the Earl of Essex. It was said of him, 'He carries his love and his hatred on his forehead.'

In 1598, a German visitor described her as, "fair, but wrinkled; her eyes small, jet-black and pleasant; her nose a little hooked; her lips narrow and her teeth black; her hair was of an auburn colour, but false..." But the men around Elizabeth, her courtiers and councillors, were compelled to maintain the fiction of her youth and beauty, showering her with compliments and praise.

In 1598, things came to a head between the Queen and Essex. When she refused one of his demands, he deliberately turned his back on her. "Go to the devil!" she shouted, and slapped him. "Get you gone and be hanged."

Essex reached for his sword. "I neither can nor will put up with so great an affront," he retorted. A lord stepped between them before Essex could strike, and he stormed from the room. Most people thought the Queen would imprison him in the Tower. She did nothing, but their relationship never quite recovered.

On August 4, 1598, William Cecil died, breaking Elizabeth's last link with her past. She felt alone, without her trusted friends, or even her old enemies, for a month later Philip of Spain died too.

The following month, news came of trouble in Ireland. The Earl of Tyrone, a rebel Irish leader, had ambushed the English army, killing over a thousand men. He had united Ireland behind him, demanding the departure of the English troops. Essex, now forgiven, begged to be made Lord Deputy of Ireland, and was given the leadership of the greatest army of Elizabeth's reign.

Many were relieved to see Essex go, believing his power was now due as much to Elizabeth's fear of him as her love. But Essex's Irish campaign went from bad to worse. Knowing he would never be able to defeat Tyrone, he ignored Elizabeth's orders and made a secret truce with the Irish leader.

A picture showing the meeting of Essex and the Earl of Tyrone in Ireland, in 1599

Then he decided to march on London to demand that Robert Cecil and his faction be removed from Court, insisting he meant no harm to the Queen. But he must have changed his mind, for at the last minute, he abandoned his army, rode to Westminster, and burst into the Queen's bedchamber to explain what he had done. From that moment on, the Court waited tensely to see what would happen.

Although the Queen seemed pleased to see Essex at first, she could not forgive him for the disaster in Ireland, or the way he had disobeyed her orders. She gradually stripped him of all his positions. Meanwhile, Essex plotted his revenge. He built up an army of outcasts, deserters from the army, Puritans, ardent Catholics – anyone who had a grudge against the Queen – arrogantly assuming that the public would rise up to fight for him.

On February 8, he gathered his friends and soldiers and marched through London. But, instead of flocking to his side, the people of London stayed indoors. Realising, too late, that no one was joining him, Essex fled home. Elizabeth sent soldiers to arrest him and take him to the Tower. This time, she didn't hestitate to sign the death warrant.

Elizabeth never showed any regret for his death. He had, after all, threatened her crown and her popularity. But she wore the ring he had given her for the rest of her life.

The Court was now much more peaceful, but Elizabeth complained to the French ambassador that, "she was tired of life, for nothing now contented her or gave her any enjoyment." There was a sense that the country was tired of having an old woman as its queen.

But she still possessed some of her old magic, making a 'golden speech' to her MPs in November, 1601.

Painted several years after her death, this portrait shows Elizabeth in old age.

"And though you have had and may have mightier and wiser princes sitting in this seat, yet you never had nor shall have any that will love you better..."

Trumpets sounded at the end of her speech, and she was thanked for, "the happy and quiet and most sweet and comfortable peace we have long enjoyed."

At sixty-nine, the Queen still rode and went for long walks, but she rarely danced in public. She had trouble with her eyesight, and sometimes with her memory, too. She still refused to name her successor, but it was now generally accepted by her councillors that the crown would pass to Mary Stuart's son, King James VI of Scotland.

In February, 1603, Elizabeth's cousin and close friend, the Countess of Nottingham, died. The Queen was at her deathbed, and afterwards fell into a deep depression. "All the fabric of my reign, little by little, is beginning to fail," she wrote to Henry IV of France.

Elizabeth's funeral procession – people wept as it passed

By March she had taken to her room. She lay on cushions on the floor and wouldn't speak to anyone. "The Queen grew worse and worse, because she would be so, none about her being able to persuade her to go to bed," wrote her cousin, Robert Carey.

On the evening of March 23, feeling her life begin to slip away, she asked for the Archbishop to come and pray at her bedside. Shortly before three o'clock the next morning, Elizabeth breathed her last.

She had reigned for forty-five years, given her country peace and stability and seen it become one of the great powers of Europe. She had ruled as a woman in a man's world, gained the love of her people and guided her country safely through a time of religious upheaval and rebellion. The great Elizabethan age was over.

ACKNOWLEDGEMENTS

© **akg-images** p30, pp62-3 (British Library); © **Alamy** p3 (Mooch Travel), pp32-3 (Michael Wald); © **Bridgeman Art Library** p1 (Private Collection/The Stapleton Collection), p4 (Walker Art Gallery, National Museums Liverpool), p5 (Hever Castle, Kent), p6 (National Portrait Gallery, London, UK), p7 (FORBES Magazine Collection, New York), p9 (Look and Learn/Elgar Collection), pp10-11 (Royal Collection Trust, (c) Her Majesty Queen Elizabeth, II, 2014), p12 (National Portrait Gallery, London/Roger-Viollet, Paris), pp14-15 (Society of Antiquaries of London), p18 (The Trustees of the Weston Park Foundation), p20 (The Fine Art Society, London), p21 (Society of Antiquaries of London), p22 (Houses of Parliament, Westminster, London), p24 (Private Collection/The Stapleton Collection), p26 (Trustees of the Bedford Estate, Woburn Abbey), p35 (National Portrait Gallery, London, UK), p36 (Private Collection), p38 (Nottingham City Museums and Galleries (Nottingham Castle)), p42 (Private Collection/The Stapleton Collection), p44 (Christie's Images), p45 (Private Collection), p47(b) (Culture and Sport Glasgow Museums), p50 (Berkeley Castle, Gloucestershire), pp52-3 (Private Collection/Rafael Valls Gallery, London, UK), p54(m) (Kunsthistorisches Museum, Vienna, Austria), p59 (Private Collection/Ken Welsh), p61 (Corsham Court, Wiltshire); © **Corbis** p17, p25 (National Gallery, London), p43 (Heritage Images), p48, p49 (Fine Art Photographic Library), p54 (Joel W. Rogers), p57 (Heritage Images); © **Getty Images** p28 (Hulton Archive), p29 (Stock Montage/Archive Photos), p55(m) (De Agostini); © **Mary Evans Picture Library** p41 (INTERFOTO / Sammlung Rauch), p47(t); © **The National Archives** ref. EXT11/25 p27; © **National Maritime Museum, Greenwich, London** cover, p18; © **Shutterstock RF** p2 & p55(bm) (Cranach); © By kind permission of **Viscount de L'Isle** from his private collection at Penshurst Place, Kent, England p37; © **The Weiss Gallery, London** p38

Internet links

To find out more about the life and times of Queen Elizabeth I, go to the Usborne Quicklinks website at **www.usborne.com/quicklinks** and type in the title of this book. Please follow the internet safety guidelines at the Usborne Quicklinks website.

Edited by Jane Chisholm
Digital manipulation by Keith Funivall

First published in 2014 by Usborne Publishing Ltd., Usborne House, 83-85 Saffron Hill, London EC1N 8RT, England. www.usborne.com